CATCHING THE
JIGGLYPUFF
THIEF

CATCHING THE JIGGLYPUFF THIEF

UNOFFICIAL ADVENTURES FOR POKÉMON GO PLAYERS

Book One

ALex PoLan

Sky Pony Press
New York

First Edition

This is a work of fiction. Names, characters, places, and incidents are from the author's imagination, and used fictitiously.

Sky Pony Press books may be purchased in bulk at special discounts for sales promotion, corporate gifts, fund-raising, or educational purposes. Special editions can also be created to specifications. For details, contact the Special Sales Department, Sky Pony Press, 307 West 36th Street, 11th Floor, New York, NY 10018 or info@skyhorsepublishing.com.

Visit our website at www.skyponypress.com.

Books, authors, and more at SkyPonyPressBlog.com.

10 9 8 7 6 5 4 3 2 1

Library of Congress Cataloging-in-Publication Data is available on file.

Special thanks to Erin L. Falligant.

Cover illustration by Jarrett Williams
Cover colors by Jeremy Lawson
Cover design by Brian Peterson

Print ISBN: 978-1-5107-2157-9
Ebook ISBN: 978-1-5107-2161-6

Printed in Canada

CHAPTER 1

"Ooh, look, they planted flowers at the entrance to the park!" gushed Mom. "See the flower garden, Ethan?"

"Sure, I see it." What Ethan *wished* he could see was the Pokémon that had popped up on his phone just a second ago. Where'd it go? Had he passed it already?

"Here," whispered his younger sister, Devin. She used her finger to spin the map on his screen and then tapped on the yellow Pokémon. A Pidgey appeared, hovering just over a daisy in the flower garden.

Ethan sighed. He wished it were something

more powerful, like a Pidgeotto. But no such luck! He flung a Poké Ball and easily captured the bird-like Pokémon.

"Oh, it's a Pidgey!" announced Dad—late to the scene, as usual.

"What's that, dear?" asked Mom.

Dad glanced up from his phone and cleared his throat. "I said it's so *pretty*. The flower garden, I mean." He sometimes pretended he wasn't all that into Pokémon GO, but Ethan knew better.

As Devin squatted to center the Pidgey on her phone screen, Ethan said, "Don't you have, like, seventeen of those already?"

She tucked a strand of red hair behind her ear and nodded. "Yup, I have a whole flock of them. And now"—she swiped her Poké Ball—"I have one more. Gotcha!"

"Why don't you trade some to Professor Willow for candy?" asked Ethan. "Or evolve some of them to make them more powerful?"

Devin scrunched up her freckled nose. "Trade my Pidgeys? No way. They're too cute. Look!"

She showed Ethan a photo she'd taken of the Pidgey. The Pokémon was perched right on the toe of Mom's sneaker.

"Ha! That's a good one," he said. Devin also had photos of Pokémon sitting on people's shoulders and in the palms of their hands. Sometimes his sister didn't even catch the Pokémon. She was too busy taking pictures of them!

Mom caught sight of the photo, too, and she shook her foot as if the Pokémon were really there.

As Devin hurried on ahead, admiring her newest Pidgey, Ethan pulled his mother aside. "It's time to get Devin a *real* pet, don't you think?" he asked.

The truth was, Ethan wanted a pet even more than his animal-loving sister did. He'd been pushing for a dog for, like, two years. *But the way things are going this summer, we'll probably end up with a pet pigeon,* he thought with a sigh.

Mom ignored the pet question, as usual. "Let's keep moving, sweetie," she said, jogging in place. "I've got an egg to hatch. Just another half kilometer to go!"

Mom never actually caught Pokémon, no matter how many times Ethan tried to teach her how. She preferred to hatch her own—for the exercise, because she didn't get much of that in her job as a realtor. Her motto was: "You play the game your way, I'll play mine."

Some eggs hatched after a short walk. Others took longer. So Mom had been leading family walks around their Newville neighborhood every night, ever since they'd discovered Pokémon GO. "Next stop, the Little Library!" she announced.

The Little Library looked like a birdhouse, a wooden box on a stand where people left books they'd read for other people to take home to read. But when Ethan looked at it, all he saw was the bright blue PokéStop on his phone. He spun the Photo Disc to see which items would pop up tonight.

One Poké Ball, then two, and then three appeared in little bubbles. And the last item was a yellow, diamond-shaped item. "Yes! A Revive!" he cheered, tapping the bubbles to collect his items.

"Really?" said Devin. "How'd you get that?" She stared at her phone, as if waiting for the Revive to appear.

"I'm a Level-Five Trainer now, remember?" said Ethan. He'd just leveled up that afternoon, but already, Level Five seemed pretty sweet. He couldn't wait to join a Team Mystic gym and start training his Pokémon!

Mom opened up the door to the Little Library to check out the books. It was a rule of hers— they had to look every night to see which books were new. But Ethan noticed she was spinning her Photo Disc at the same time.

"Ooh, an egg!" she announced. "Now I just need another incubator . . ."

As Devin skipped up the sidewalk to her friend

Gianna's house, Ethan glanced hopefully at the front door. Gianna's older brother, Carlo, was the neighborhood Pokémon GO expert. He was only fourteen—four years older than Ethan—but he had already reached Level Twelve. And he was the Gym Leader at Dottie's Doughnuts, the Team Mystic gym on Main Street.

He's probably at the doughnut shop right now, training his Pokémon, thought Ethan. But he secretly hoped Carlo would step out that door and go Pokémon hunting with them. At Level Twelve, he was always spotting rare Pokémon that no one else could see, and Ethan liked to tag along—at least, when Carlo would let him.

When the front door jiggled, Ethan held his breath. *Carlo?*

Nope. Gianna popped out instead, her dark curls bouncing around her head. She pulled on her lucky cap, which made her look like a giant bug because it had two springy antennae on top. She said it helped her find Bug-type Pokémon—her favorite. But Ethan wasn't so sure about that.

"Can I hunt for Pokémon with you guys?" she asked, not waiting for an answer.

"Sure, Gia!" said Devin. She bent over her phone, logging out of it. Gianna's parents wouldn't buy her a phone till she turned ten—a year from now—but Devin always seemed happy to share hers.

As Gianna punched in her user name, Ethan glanced at the screen. "Your Trainer name is 'Giadude99'?"

"Yeah. Get it?" asked Gianna. "It's like Geodude, but with 'Gia' instead."

Devin laughed. "Oh, I get it. Your avatar is pretty cute, too."

When the phone vibrated in Gianna's hand, Devin peeked at the screen—and then shrunk back. "Ick, an ugly Rattata. You don't have to catch him, Gia. Just run! Tap the button at the top."

"Why wouldn't you catch a Rattata?" asked Ethan. "I thought you wanted to catch them all!"

"Because I don't like Rattata. If I don't like ugly ratlike Pokémon, I don't have to catch them," Devin said matter-of-factly. "And if I *like* my flock of Pidgey, I don't have to trade them."

Ethan ignored that last part. "So if a super-powerful Rattata with the world's highest Combat Power crossed your screen, you wouldn't even *try* to catch it?" he asked.

Devin shrugged. "You play your way, I'll play mine."

Wow. Ethan couldn't believe she had just used Mom's line on him! But before he could protest, he saw Gianna using her finger to spin the Poké Ball on the screen. It started to sparkle. Then she flung it at the Rattata—and hit it dead center.

The ball bounced off its forehead with a *plink!* and sucked the Pokémon right up.

"Bam! You got it on the first shot!" said Ethan. "With a curveball, even. Did Carlo teach you that?"

Gianna shook her head. "He doesn't even let me play with him."

I know the feeling, thought Ethan. He caught the Rattata, too, with a normal shot—except it took him three tries. Then he shot one last look at Carlo's front door and walked on.

At the next PokéStop, which was a trailhead sign for the Pheasant Ranch Nature Preserve, Ethan collected a few more items. This time, he was given six Poké Balls instead of the usual three or four. Level Five was really paying off!

But as he scanned his phone for Pokémon, he got the creepy feeling that someone was following him down the sidewalk. One glance over his shoulder told him who it was: Brayden. Ethan would recognize that white-blonde head of hair anywhere.

When Brayden saw Ethan looking, he dropped down beside his golden retriever puppy, fiddling with the dog's collar.

Ethan sped up, zooming past Devin and Gianna. "Why are you going so fast?" asked Devin. "Do you see something?" She studied her screen.

"Brayden the Great is following me," he whispered.

"Wait, aren't you and Brayden friends?" asked Gianna.

"We *were,* before he stole my Poké Ball hat and totally denied it."

"Your new black baseball cap?" asked Devin.

"Yeah, that one. Then he stole my idea for the perfect dog name!"

Gianna looked back at Brayden's puppy. "What's her name?"

"Lickitung, after the Pokémon. Licks, for short," said Ethan. "That was *my* name for a dog, if we ever get one."

"I would have named the dog Twinkie," said Devin with a grin. "She's golden on the outside, but pure sweetness on the inside!"

Gianna laughed, but Ethan just kept talking— he couldn't seem to stop. "Brayden gets his mom to buy him lucky Pokémon eggs, incense, and lures so he can get more experience. Whatever happened to *earning* experience points?"

"Wow," said Devin. "You're really down on Brayden."

"Well, he bragged about getting to Level Five before me. And he joined Team Valor, of course—they're all about being the best. So if he's the best, why is he following *me*? He probably wants to see which Pokémon I catch so that he can catch them, too."

Devin cocked her head. "Wait, isn't that kind of what you do with Carlo?"

Ethan sighed. Sometimes his sister just didn't get it. "Why don't you go capture another Pidgey or something?" he grumbled.

She shrugged. "Okay, maybe I will."

As she walked away with Gianna, Ethan looked back at Brayden, who was bold enough to be wearing the Poké Ball cap right then. *MY cap,* thought Ethan. As his eyes trailed down to the puppy, his heart ached. *Some kids get whatever they want. The rest of us have to work so hard for it!*

He sighed and kept walking. He had Pokémon to catch and experience points to earn.

Suddenly, Mom squealed from up ahead. "I hatched my egg!"

"Which Pokémon did you get?" Devin cried, running to join her. "Let me see!"

"Looks like a . . . Jiggle Puff."

"You mean a Jigglypuff?" asked Devin. "My favorite!"

Ethan shook his head. It seemed like every new

Pokémon was Devin's favorite. But Jigglypuff *was* a rare one. Devin had somehow caught the pink Pokémon last weekend, when she and Dad were sitting outside Dottie's Doughnuts.

"Yes, I guess it is a Jigglypuff," said Mom. "Now I'd better hurry and get another egg in the incubator."

She fiddled with her phone and then took off walking again—even faster this time.

Ethan hurried after her, mostly to get away from Brayden. But Dad stayed behind, wandering along the tree line of the nature preserve. "Tell your mother I'll catch up," he called. "I spy a Caterpie . . ."

"Moving grass!" Devin announced, sprinting toward a field up ahead as she tapped her phone screen. "It looks like an Ivysaur—or maybe even a Venusaur. It's just a couple of footsteps away!"

Ethan and Gianna followed on her heels. Devin was pretty good at rustling up Pokémon. Plus, she was the only one who used the app's tracking feature to tell what sorts of Pokémon were in the area.

As they ran, Ethan crossed his fingers, hoping it really was a Venusaur. He wondered what else they might find in the field. *A Victreebel? Ooh, or how about a Scyther?* His heart raced with the possibilities.

That's when he heard a howl from behind, and the sound of branches breaking.

Ethan whirled around. "Dad?"

The sidewalk was completely empty.

CHAPTER 2

Ethan sprinted toward the place where he had last seen Dad. Just through the row of trees lining the edge of the nature preserve, he stopped short. A steep ravine stretched down below.

"Dad?"

There he was at the very bottom, brushing off his shorts. "I'm alright!" he called up with a sheepish laugh. "Nothing to see down here, folks!"

Ethan breathed a sigh of relief. If Dad was joking, he must be okay.

Mom wasn't so sure. She stepped carefully down the side of the ravine, and then helped Dad climb back up. He was missing a sandal, and his shirt was torn.

When Ethan saw a trickle of blood running down Dad's knee, his chest tightened. So he did what Dad would do—he cracked a joke. "I hope you at least caught a Caterpie while you were down there," he said.

Mom shot Ethan a look, but Dad just laughed. "Afraid not," he said. When he tried to check his phone, Mom yanked it right out of his hand.

"I think that's enough Pokémon hunting for one night," she said. "Good thing we're close to home." She magically produced a tissue from some sleeve or pocket and started dabbing at Dad's bloody knee.

They were a block away from the bus stop, which was also a PokéStop. Every night when they reached it, Dad would declare, "Well, I guess the bus stops here!" That was when Ethan and Devin would start begging for more time to hunt Pokémon on their own.

Or to train my Pokémon, Ethan thought excitedly. He'd been waiting to reach Level Five for two weeks now. He didn't want to wait even one more day before heading to a Team Mystic gym. Was there time to go to Dottie's Doughnuts tonight?

When he asked Mom, she said what she always said to him and Devin: "Stay together. And be home in half an hour." Then she added a new warning: "Watch where you're going, too. Learn from your father's mistakes!"

Dad started limping, as if to drive home the point. As he followed Mom down the sidewalk, he looked a little lost—maybe because he didn't have his phone to look at. *But he'll be a whole lot safer that way*, thought Ethan.

"Ready to go to the doughnut shop?" he asked Devin.

She said yes, like he knew she would. Devin wasn't a Level-Five Trainer yet, but she had a wicked sweet tooth. She never turned down the chance to go to Dottie's—especially in the evening, when Dottie gave out day-old doughnuts for free.

"Can I come, too?" Gianna asked hopefully. "Carlo is probably there. And there might be a Butterfree fluttering outside the shop. He said he saw one last night!"

The three of them set off for Dottie's Doughnuts. It was a perfect summer night, and Pokémon were *everywhere*.

Devin let Gianna catch a Spearow on her phone. She made it look so easy!

"Excellent throw!" the screen read, and Gianna

was awarded a hundred extra experience points for her shot.

"How do you do that?" asked Ethan.

She shrugged. "Practice, I guess."

As they neared the library, Devin and Ethan put their phones away. The library was a Team Mystic gym, just like the doughnut shop. But Ethan had heard that the librarian, Mrs. Applegate, shooed away any kids who tried to play there. She believed in *books*, not video games or apps.

There was Mrs. Applegate now! Ethan ducked his head and gave a little wave as she stepped out to sweep the front walk. Then he followed Devin and Gianna across the street to the doughnut shop.

Just as Gianna had suspected, Carlo was sitting on the wooden bench out front. He had on gaming gloves, and his dark hair was angled down to a perfect point above his upturned jacket collar.

I'll never be that cool, thought Ethan. *Not in a million years.*

He walked by slowly, hoping Carlo would look up. When he finally did, Ethan waved, but Carlo seemed to be looking at a Pokémon on his phone instead.

Ethan quickly stopped waving and ran his hand over his sandy-brown hair instead. Then he approached the PokéStop across from the bench. It was a bike rack shaped like a long metal caterpillar.

Ethan spun the Photo Disc and collected a few Poké Balls.

When a purple spray bottle of Potion popped up, too, he almost squealed. But he held himself together, knowing Carlo was right behind him. He tapped on the bubbles to collect his items and then headed inside.

Devin and Gianna went straight to the counter, where Dottie greeted them with a tray of doughnuts. "I was hoping to have company tonight!" she said warmly, her gold earrings jingling against her cocoa-brown skin. "I've had more day-old doughnuts than I know what to do with, ever since Ivan's Ice Cream opened up across town. Help yourselves."

Normally, Ethan would have grabbed a doughnut. But tonight, he had bigger plans. He slid into a booth and tapped on the tall blue gym on his screen. Finally, he could interact with the gym instead of having Professor Willow tell him he wasn't *experienced* enough!

Dottie's Doughnuts was a Level-Two gym, which meant there were two trainers defending it. The first one was a girl Ethan didn't know: BatGirl16, with a Zubat by her side. But when Ethan swiped to the right, he found Carlo. His dark-haired avatar, named Carlozard14, stood proudly next to a Jolteon named "Sparky." And above the Pokémon, Carlo's Gym-Leader crown shone bright.

Someday, thought Ethan, *that could be mine!* He stared for a moment longer and then chose his most powerful Pokémon for battle. That choice was easy.

Ethan's Pidgeotto appeared on screen, ready to fight the Zubat. It was the first time Ethan had seen his trainer name in battle: DogBoy918. He grinned and prepared to attack.

But Zubat had already struck! It bit Pidgeotto, who squawked and reeled backward.

Ethan quickly tapped the screen. "Attack, Pidgeotto! What are you waiting for?" He got off one shot, but Zubat came back fighting.

The battle was halfway over before Ethan even remembered that he could dodge attacks. *Swipe left and right*, he reminded himself. But it was too late!

Zubat squealed as it delivered its Special Attack, the Poison Fang. And Pidgeotto disappeared in a puff of smoke.

Already? thought Ethan, slumping down in his seat. He glanced at the counter to see if the girls had been watching. Luckily, they were deep into their doughnuts—and their conversation with Dottie.

"So, I have an idea for how you can sell more doughnuts," said Gianna, who was always coming up with new plans. She wiped powdered sugar off her cheek and said, "How about if you call them Pokémon GO-nuts? You could offer two GO-nuts for the price of one!"

Dottie looked confused. "GO-nuts?" She hadn't caught on to the Pokémon GO craze yet, Ethan could tell.

But Devin was so excited, she nearly dropped her doughnut. Purple sprinkles bounced across the counter. "Here's another idea," she said. "What if you bake a special doughnut that looks like a Pokémon? Maybe like a Jigglypuff!" She scrolled to a picture of the Pokémon on her phone to show Dottie.

"Hmm," said Dottie, tapping her chin. "With pink frosting and some candy eyes, maybe I could . . ."

As Ethan prepared for another battle, he tried to tune out the girls' voices. *You're not battling Jigglypuff,* he reminded himself. *You're battling Zubat.* He'd waited so long for this chance. He had to focus!

First, he had to heal his Pidgeotto, whose hit points had dropped way down. *Good thing I have a Potion,* thought Ethan, hitting the "Items" button.

After healing his favorite Pokémon, he started a new battle. This time, Ethan remembered to dodge Zubat's first attack. Pidgeotto got off a strike or two and then dodged another bite, flapping its powerful wings.

Take that, you ugly vampire! thought Ethan, madly tapping the screen.

Finally, *finally,* Zubat fainted and disappeared. *Poof!*

"Yes!" said Ethan, pumping his fist.

"Yes, what?" asked Devin. "You think the lure module is a good idea?"

"No, I won a battle!" explained Ethan.

But before he could celebrate, Sparky took Zubat's place. And that Jolteon Pokémon was fierce. He used his Thunder Shock attack against Pidgeotto over and over again, sending bolts of electricity across the screen.

I can't believe I'm battling Carlo's Pokémon! thought Ethan, looking out the window to see if Carlo was still around. The bench was empty. And by the time Ethan turned back to his screen, the battle was over.

"You lose!" the screen announced.

Still, Ethan couldn't help smiling as he walked toward the counter. "Wait, did you say something about a lure?" he asked.

Gianna nodded. "We think Dottie should add a lure to the bike rack PokéStop out front. It would bring in a lot of customers!"

"Can you teach her how, Ethan?" Devin asked.

He shrugged. "I don't exactly have a lure module sitting in my item bag. They cost a hundred PokéCoins, and I won't get a free one until I'm at least a Level-Eight Trainer!"

"No, no," said Dottie, raising her hand. "I'll buy it myself—I mean, if I can. I don't know much about this Pokémon GO thing." Her forehead creased with worry.

"We can help you," Ethan said quickly.

He showed her how to download the app on her phone and create an account. Then he showed her the shop where she could purchase the lure module. "But don't use it tonight!" he said. "It only works for thirty minutes. You want to use it when lots of people are going to be around."

"Like tomorrow," said Gianna. "Saturday would be a good day, right?"

"Yes!" said Devin. "You'll sell a ton of Jigglypuffs on a Saturday."

"Tomorrow?" said Dottie, checking the clock. "I guess Saturday morning would be good. Maybe ten o'clock? But I'd better get busy baking if I'm going to be ready by then!" She pulled a hairnet over her cropped gray curls.

Ethan checked the clock, too. "Oh, we gotta get home," he said to Devin. "It's been a half hour already!"

"We'll be back tomorrow," Devin promised Dottie. "I'll make a sign for the Jigglypuffs. I'm so excited!"

Dottie looked more nervous than excited. But she smiled and said, "Thanks, kids. Can you lock the door on the way out, Devin? Just flip the little knob."

Ethan headed out first, with the girls close behind. But as they stepped onto the sidewalk, he heard Devin whisper, "Don't look now. *Don't move.* There's a Beedrill sitting on the bike rack!"

CHAPTER 3

Ethan pulled out his phone to catch the buzzing Beedrill, which loomed large on his screen. It glared at him with its red eyes, daring him to take a shot.

As he held his finger on the Poké Ball, he waited for the circle around the Pokémon to shrink down to size. The circle was an orangish red, which was never a good sign.

Ethan's first Poké Ball bounced right over the Beedrill. The second struck it dead center and captured it. "Yes!" shouted Ethan.

Then the ball wiggled, and the Pokémon buzzed right back out. "So you want to play that game, huh?" Ethan muttered, trying again.

"Do you want help?" asked Gianna.

"No, I've got this," said Ethan. He tried to use Gianna's curveball approach, but he missed the Pokémon entirely. *Oops!* He turned his body so that Gianna couldn't see the screen.

With his fourth Poké Ball, he held his breath. He waited until *after* the Beedrill had done its dodge move. Then Ethan flung the ball.

"Bam! Yes! Gotcha!"

Except he didn't. The Beedrill broke loose again and disappeared in a puff of smoke.

"No!" Ethan sunk down onto his knees. "Beedrill is going to be the end of me, I swear."

"I caught it," Devin said proudly, holding up her phone. There was Beedrill hovering over the seat of a bike.

"You didn't catch it," Ethan corrected her. "You took a picture—that's different."

"It's a pretty good photo though, isn't it?" said Gianna, grinning.

Ethan had to admit that it was. It looked like Beedrill was actually riding the bike. "I wish we'd ridden *our* bikes," he said. "We're going to be late again. I hope Mom doesn't ground us!"

"Or take away our phones," added Devin, looking horrified. She took off like a shot, and Ethan and Gianna raced after her toward home.

On Saturday morning, when Ethan opened his eyes, he heard Devin arguing with Mom in the kitchen.

"But I'm going to have Jigglypuff doughnuts at Dottie's!" Devin protested.

"Doughnuts aren't a proper breakfast. And it's too early to be talking about Pokémon. Now, eat your eggs."

Ethan pushed back the covers, stretched, and then padded into the kitchen. He found Dad at the table, staring at his phone. "Are you playing already?" Ethan asked.

Dad stole a look at Mom and shook his head. "No, of course not. I'm in the middle of, um . . . sorting my contact list. See, this here is my friend Larry."

Ethan looked over Dad's shoulder. He was tapping the little pencil beside a Weedle! When the "Set Nickname" box popped up, Dad typed in the name "Larry."

Ethan choked back laughter. "Wow, um, I didn't know you had a friend named Larry."

Dad nodded. "Oh, yeah. We go way back."

Way back to when? Last night? thought Ethan. *Right before you fell in the ditch?* But he didn't say anything. Judging by the bandage on Dad's knee—and the look on Mom's face—he probably didn't need to be reminded.

It took an hour before Ethan and Devin could convince Mom to let them head to the doughnut shop. They hopped on their bikes to make up for lost time. Strapped to the bar of Devin's bike was her sign for Dottie's window, rolled up into a long tube.

When they reached the shop, it was already almost ten. Ethan expected to see trays of pink Jigglypuffs on the counter. Instead, he saw only Dottie, dabbing at her tear-stained face with a napkin.

"Oh, kids," she said. "I'm glad to see you. Something awful happened last night. Someone broke into the shop!"

"What?" asked Ethan. "No way! What did they steal? Did they get into the cash register?"

When Dottie shook her head, her earrings jingled. "No, thank goodness. But they stole a tray of Jigglypuffs. Right off the counter!"

Ethan blew out a breath of relief, but Devin looked devastated. "Not the Jigglypuffs! What about your big sale today?"

Dottie shrugged. "I guess we'll have to do it another day."

"Do what another day?" asked Gianna, pushing through the front door.

After Dottie filled her in, Gianna leaned against the counter, resting her chin in her hands. "That stinks. Setting the lure was such a good idea, too!"

"I know," said Devin. "I brought the sign and everything!" She unrolled the scroll of paper to reveal a sign made from one of her photos. Jigglypuff was sitting on a plate beside a cup of coffee.

Above the photo, Devin had written in big letters: GET YOUR JIGGLYPUFFS AT DOTTIE'S DOUGHNUTS. TWO POKÉMON GO-NUTS FOR THE PRICE OF ONE!

Looking at the sign that Devin had worked so hard on, Ethan felt a sudden surge of anger. "We should do the sale anyway," he said. "We're not going to let some dumb thief ruin our day, are we?"

Gianna followed his lead. "No! Maybe we can just set the lure a little later, like at noon. Can we, Dottie?"

She shook her head. "I don't have enough doughnuts—I mean, Pokémon GO-nuts—to sell. I'd have to make more, and there's just no time!"

"What if we help you?" asked Gianna.

Devin perked right up. "Yeah, we can help!"

Ethan wasn't so sure. But he was willing to pitch in, if it would make Dottie feel better.

She turned and looked at the kids, one by one, and finally said, "Okay. We can try." She even smiled, just a little.

Soon the four of them were busily making Jigglypuffs. Gianna helped mix up the batter before Dottie fried the balls of dough. Ethan was in charge of adding food coloring to the frosting to make it the perfect shade of pink. And Devin stuck candy eyes and chocolate-kiss ears onto the frosted doughnuts.

By the time they were done, Ethan realized something. He had been at the doughnut shop gym for two hours, and he hadn't trained his Pokémon. He hadn't even thought about it—not once!

When he pulled out his phone, Dottie misunderstood. "Are you going to show me how to set that lure module now?" she asked brightly.

"Um, yes. But let's do it on your phone, since you already bought the lure." It took a lot of strength for Ethan to slide his own phone back into his pocket.

"We'd better hurry!" said Devin, washing her hands. "It's already hot out. If we wait too long, people will want ice cream instead of doughnuts."

Ethan caught the hurt expression that flickered across Dottie's face. But he knew Devin was right.

They were running out of time. So he showed Dottie how to set the lure module on the bike rack PokéStop, right through the glass window.

Then he pulled out his own phone, and was happy to see the pink petals falling all around the PokéStop on his map. He knew other Pokémon GO players could see them, too—even from three or four blocks away!

Ethan had never set a lure before. "I sure hope it works," he whispered, smiling.

Devin and Gianna had already stepped out front, scanning the street for Pokémon—and customers. When Ethan's phone vibrated, he checked the screen. A Spearow was sitting next to the PokéStop! He took a moment to capture it through the window.

"Is that a Pokémon?" asked Dottie. "I don't understand. I thought the lure model was supposed to draw in customers, not Pokémon!"

"That's how it works," Ethan explained. "It lures Pokémon. Like, one every few minutes. And because there are lots of Pokémon here to catch, *people* show up, too. At least, I hope they will!"

"Oh! We'd better get this up, then," said Dottie, reaching for Devin's sign on the counter.

Ethan pressed the sign against the window while Dottie taped the corners. Then he hurried outside before another Pokémon showed up.

As soon as he stepped onto the sidewalk, he stopped short. The street suddenly seemed crowded, *very* crowded. He looked left and then right. People were coming, alright. And lots of them!

"Dottie!" he shouted back through the door. "Get ready!"

CHAPTER 4

"**M**ay I help you?" asked Ethan, pulling on a new pair of plastic gloves.

The doughnut shop was so crowded that he and Devin were helping Dottie serve customers. Gianna was pitching in, too, refilling the napkin dispenser by the coffeepot.

"Can I have a Jigglypuff, please?" asked a little boy, standing on tiptoe to see over the counter.

Ethan reached for the tray in the glass case and saw that there were only two Jigglypuffs left. "You can have one of the very last ones," he told the boy, whose eyes lit up.

"We're going to have to start pushing other

doughnuts," Ethan whispered to Devin as Dottie rung up the sale. "And I think you'd better take down your Jigglypuff sign!"

While Devin pushed through the crowd to pull the sign from the window, Ethan took a good look at the doughnuts that were left in the case. When the next customer stepped up, he cleared his throat and said, "Would you like to try a Long John? Or how about a cream puff? Baked fresh this morning!"

By the time the crowd thinned out, Dottie's case was nearly empty. She sank down into one of the booths and sighed happily. "That was really something, kids," she said. "I'm pooped!"

"The lure module was a success!" said Gianna, squeezing into the booth beside Dottie.

"So were the Jigglypuffs. What a great day!" said Devin, sitting across from her.

Dottie nodded, but Ethan saw the moment when her face began to fall.

"It sure didn't start out that way, though," she said. "I'm almost afraid to leave the shop this afternoon. What if someone breaks in again tonight?"

With that, the happy mood in the bakery popped like a PokéStop bubble.

"I wish we could figure out who the thief is," Ethan murmured.

Dottie sighed. "I should have installed a security camera way back when, like everyone told me to."

"Maybe there's another way to catch the thief," suggested Gianna. She tugged on one of the bug antennae on her cap, as if it helped her think. "Were there any clues?"

Dottie shrugged. "A missing tray of Jigglypuffs. That's it."

"Which door did they break in through?" asked Ethan. "Maybe they left fingerprints!"

"That's what I don't understand!" said Dottie. "They didn't break in at all. The lock wasn't damaged, and no glass was broken. Maybe someone has a copy of my key?" Her forehead wrinkled with worry.

Suddenly, Devin's did, too. "Oh, no," she whispered. "I think I forgot to lock the door last night. Because we saw that Beedrill, remember, Ethan?"

She stood up, fishing her phone out of her pocket. "I got a picture of the Beedrill." She showed it to Dottie, as if that would somehow make up for the unlocked door and the missing doughnuts.

Then Devin pulled her phone back. "Wait, there's something else in the picture. Look!"

Ethan glanced at the photo. "Yeah, you already showed me that. It's Beedrill riding a bike." He was still bitter about the way that buglike Pokémon had burst out of the Poké Ball—twice!

"But whose bike is it?" asked Devin. "Maybe whoever owns it saw something, or knows something about the crime!"

Silence fell over the table as Ethan and the others chewed on that thought.

Ethan studied the bicycle. He couldn't see very much of it in the photo, but he could tell it was a bright red bike with the word MILE on it. Or was that part of another word?

"If someone parked their bike here on the sidewalk, they could have overheard us talking about the Jigglypuffs," he agreed. "That person might even have come back later to *steal* them!"

"Hold on, now," said Dottie, raising her hand. "Let's not go accusing anybody until we have all the facts."

"Right," said Gianna, her antennae jiggling as she nodded. "Whoever owns that bike is just a person of interest—wanted for questioning, I mean. We have to calmly analyze the situation."

"Huh?" said Devin. "Have you been watching a lot of crime shows?"

"No, she's quoting the Team Mystic motto," explained Ethan. "And I guess that motto is a good way for us to try to solve the crime, too. So . . . who's with me?" He held out his hand in front of him, palm down.

Gianna put her hand on Ethan's. "I'm in."

Devin slapped hers on top. "Me, too!"

Dottie smiled. "Alright, then. As long as you promise to *calmly* analyze the situation."

"We will," said Ethan. "Go, Team Mystic!"

"Team Mystic!" the girls repeated.

And with that, the Case of the Stolen Jigglypuffs had officially begun.

By the time Devin and Ethan made it back to the house, rain was pouring down in buckets. So much for searching the neighborhood for a red bike!

Instead, Ethan flopped down onto his bed, searching through all the Pokémon he had caught or hatched. Could he evolve some of them? Now that he was training at the gym, he needed more powerful Pokémon.

He had already evolved a Pidgey to a Pidgeotto. That was pretty easy—it only required twelve Pidgey Candy. *What else do I have lots of?* he wondered, studying his list of captured Pokémon.

He sorted the list by name, and then he saw it—a whole pack of Rattata. "There's a gazillion of them!" he said out loud, scrolling through the list.

He tapped on the one with the highest Combat Power and checked out its stats. Could he evolve it?

Yes, he could! The Rattata needed twenty-five Candy to evolve into a Raticate, and Ethan had forty-two of them. He pressed the "Evolve" button and sat back to watch the show.

Rattata snapped at him from the black screen, until he was lifted off the ground in a flash of light. The brilliant ball swirled and sparkled. Finally, a fierce Raticate sprang out, snarling and ready for battle.

"Cool!" shouted Ethan. That Raticate was exactly what he needed—a nasty-looking Pokémon that other trainers would be afraid to take on.

I can't wait to take this bad boy to Dottie's, he thought, setting down his phone.

"Ew!" someone said from behind, making Ethan jump.

When he looked up, Devin was standing at the foot of his bed, staring at his phone. "What are you doing with that big, ugly rat?" she asked, pointing at the screen.

"It's Raticate!" he said. "I evolved my Rattata, like *you* should do with your Pidgey."

Devin narrowed her eyes. "Not gonna happen."

"Ooh, I just thought of the perfect nickname for my Raticate," said Ethan, grabbing his phone. "I'm going to name it Devin."

"What? You can't do that!" she said, trying to pull the phone out of his hands.

"Sure I can. If Dad can call his Weedle 'Larry,' I can call my Raticate 'Devin.'"

"Your dad did *what?*" Mom was suddenly standing in the doorway.

Before Ethan could answer, he heard Dad clear his throat in the hallway. "Hurry, dear," he said quickly. "It stopped raining! We'd better get our walk in before it starts up again."

"Yes, we'd better," said Mom, checking her watch. "Are you kids ready?"

"Ready!" said Devin. She leaned closer to Ethan and whispered, "Time to keep our eyes peeled for you know what."

He cocked his head. "For a Raticate named Devin?"

"No!" she scolded, sounding just like Mom. "For red bikes."

Ethan laughed. "Oh, yeah. I almost forgot. Team Mystic?" He held out his hand.

"Team Mystic," said Devin, putting her hand on top.

"How about if we walk someplace new?" asked

Mom, lacing up her sneakers. "Maybe the lake on the other side of town? Or the trail through Pheasant Ranch Nature Preserve?"

"No!" Devin and Ethan said at the same time.

We can't look for the red bike at the lake or in a nature preserve, thought Ethan. *Of all the nights for Mom to try to change things up . . .*

Mom's eyes widened. "Well, alright then," she said. "Another night, maybe. But be prepared to keep up, kids. I'm going for my silver Jogger medal."

Ethan met Devin's eyes and sighed. A silver Jogger medal required, like, a hundred kilometers of walking. That was a lot of family walks! But he was glad Mom had agreed to stick close to their neighborhood.

"Smell that fresh air," Mom said as they neared the park. "Oh, and someone must be barbecuing. Do you smell that, Ethan?" She inhaled deeply.

"Yeah, I smell it," he said. But it was hard to focus on smelling when he was trying so hard to *see*—a red bike, that is. He hurried toward the bike rack at the entrance to the park, but found only a shiny, purple bike with training wheels.

As Ethan followed his family toward the Little Library, he scanned every front yard and open garage they passed. He barely noticed when Gianna joined the group. And he ignored a wobbly

Metapod on his map because he was too busy playing detective.

"Ethan, PokéStop!" Mom hollered, pulling him out of his thoughts. She was standing by the Pheasant Ranch trailhead sign. "Are you kids sure you don't want to hike the trail?"

Gianna looked torn. "There are probably lots of Bug-type Pokémon in there. But . . ."

"But we should stick to our usual walk," said Devin quickly. "Right, Ethan?"

Before he could answer, he heard yipping from across the street. *Brayden and Licks,* he thought. *Again.*

Except when Ethan looked, he saw that Brayden *wasn't* walking the dog tonight. He held the dog's leash and was slowly riding alongside it. On a bicycle.

A very *red* bicycle.

CHAPTER 5

"You know, Mom," Ethan said carefully, "you and Dad should hike the trail. I can tell you really want to, and it'll help you earn that silver Jogger medal! Devin, Gianna, and I were hoping to hang out here on the block and search for special Pokémon called . . ."

"Weedle," said Devin quickly, checking the tracker on her phone.

"Um, yeah," said Ethan, wishing his sister had been a *little* more creative. "Weedle."

Dad winked and said, "If you run into my friend Larry, say hi!"

Mom cocked her head at that, but she didn't

ask any questions. She seemed too excited about hiking the trail. "Well, thank you, Ethan. We'll be back in a jiff. Till then, remember to . . ."

"We know, Mom," said Ethan. "We'll stick together—and we'll watch where we're going. I promise."

She nodded and hurried off down the trail, checking her phone pedometer as she went.

"What now?" asked Devin, stealing a glance at Brayden.

"Now we confront him," said Ethan, narrowing his eyes. "And check out that bike."

"Okay," said Gianna, holding up her hand, "but remember what we promised Dottie. We'll stay calm, right? Brayden is just a person of interest."

"Right," said Ethan. "Wanted for questioning."

But a big part of him actually hoped Brayden *was* the thief. Then the girls would finally see what a jerk he could be—and understand why Ethan didn't want to hang out with him anymore!

As they turned to walk back toward Brayden, Ethan's and Devin's phones buzzed at the exact same time.

"Whoa," said Devin. "Beedrill alert!"

"Where?" Ethan spun around until he could see the Pokémon on his map. As he tapped on it and prepared to fight, he saw Devin hand her phone to Gianna.

Ethan angled his phone so that Beedrill was dead center. Then he flung his first Poké Ball.

Miss!

He flung again, just as the Beedrill flew upward. Another miss.

The third Poké Ball caught the Beedrill, but not for long. The ball wiggled and jiggled, and then it cracked open. Beedrill buzzed out—and disappeared.

"Excellent shot!" Devin cried, looking over Gianna's shoulder. "I wish I could do that. Did you catch it too, Ethan?"

He looked away. "I don't want to talk about it."

"Catch what?" someone asked from behind.

Ethan spun around and saw Brayden on his bike. Sure enough, he had his phone out, ready to catch the Pokémon they'd found for him.

Figures, thought Ethan.

Then he remembered their plan. He took a step toward Brayden to check out the frame of his bike. What he saw sent a shiver of excitement from the top of his head to the tips of his toes.

There it was, plain as day: the brand name, MILER, in bold, white letters.

Ethan got Devin's attention and gestured

toward the bike. When she saw the writing on it, her eyes grew wide.

Now it's time to catch Brayden in his lies, just like Gianna caught that Beedrill, thought Ethan.

"So, Brayden," he said, trying to ignore the cute puppy sniffing the grass at his feet, "did you have a nice walk last night—after we saw you, I mean?"

Brayden looked confused. "Walk? No. I went to my cousin's house for a sleepover. He lives in this ginormous house by the lake," he bragged.

How convenient, thought Ethan.

"So you weren't, say, at Dottie's Doughnuts last night?" He watched Brayden's cheeks, looking for any sign of blushing.

"What?" said Brayden. "No. Why are you acting so weird?"

Ethan was about to go in for the attack—he couldn't help himself!

Devin must have noticed, because she stepped in front of him. "Did you catch any Pokémon at the lake?" she asked brightly.

Brayden grinned and checked his phone. "Yeah," he said. "I caught a ton of them—way more than my cousin did. I caught Magikarp, and Poliwag . . ." He held up a photo of a Poliwag sitting on the end of a kayak.

Ethan didn't believe a word of it. Brayden

could have caught those Pokémon anytime—it didn't have to be last night. "Prove it," he spat. The words were out of his mouth the moment he thought them.

"What?" asked Brayden. "What's your problem, Ethan?"

Devin sighed. "There was a break-in at Dottie's Doughnuts last night. Someone stole doughnuts—maybe someone riding a red bike. We're just trying to figure out who."

"And you think I stole the stupid doughnuts?" asked Brayden. "Well, I didn't. I told you—I was at the lake."

"Wow, I bet you caught a bunch of rare Pokémon," Gianna said suddenly. "Can I see your Journal? It'd be cool to know which Pokémon are out there. Maybe I'll go sometime."

What's she doing? wondered Ethan. *Why is she being so nice to him?*

Brayden looked suspicious, too, until Gianna said, "I'll bet you caught so many Pokémon there, you made it to Level Six!"

Brayden puffed out his chest. "Yeah, I sure did. I'll show you everything I caught."

He tapped on his Trainer Journal and held it out for Gianna.

Oh! That's when Ethan figured out Gianna's

plan. The Journal would tell her exactly what time of day Brayden caught those Water-type Pokémon. And if he caught them last night, he *couldn't* have been at the doughnut shop, which was nowhere near water.

Smart, Ethan realized. *Why didn't I think of that?*

"Wow, that sure is a long list," said Gianna, handing back Brayden's phone.

But Ethan could tell by the expression on her face that Brayden's story checked out. He must have caught those Pokémon last night, like he said he did. So he *wasn't* at the doughnut shop.

Bummer! thought Ethan, kicking the toe of his shoe against the sidewalk.

As Brayden got back on his bike, he scowled at Ethan. "I can't believe you thought I stole dough-nuts. I'm *not* a thief."

Ethan's eyes flickered upward. "Nice Poké Ball cap," he said.

"I told you—it's not yours!" said Brayden. "My parents bought it for me."

"Did they buy you that bike, too?" asked Ethan.

Brayden furrowed his brow. "No, it's Bella's. I'm only riding it because mine got a flat this morning."

It's Bella's.

The words buzzed around Ethan's mind like a Beedrill trapped in a Poké Ball, right before it busted back out.

He knew that Brayden's older sister, Bella, was the Team Valor Gym Leader at Ivan's Ice Cream. He knew that ice cream shop was Dottie's main competition in town—and a rival gym.

And now Ethan knew something else: Bella owned the red bike that they'd spotted at the scene of the crime.

CHAPTER 6

"It's *got* to be her," said Ethan after Brayden had pedaled away. "Maybe Bella and her Team Valor friends stole the doughnuts to stop Dottie's Jigglypuff sale. They don't want her business to do well because it's a Team Mystic gym!"

"I don't know," said Devin. "Bella's pretty nice. She babysat for us once, remember?"

Gianna nodded slowly. "I agree with Devin. Bella doesn't seem like a thief. It just doesn't feel right."

"It doesn't *feel* right?" Ethan repeated. "You're starting to sound like Team Instinct! What happened to calm analysis of the situation?" He suddenly felt very much alone. *Do these two want to solve the mystery or not?* he wondered.

Gianna sighed. "Okay, you're right. We should at least check her out as a person of interest."

Devin nodded slowly. "She *does* own the bike that was in the photo."

"Okay, then," said Ethan, relieved. "I'll bet she hangs out at the ice cream shop on Sundays. Can you meet us there after church tomorrow, Gianna?"

"I think so," she said. "But I hope Dottie doesn't find out we went there. After everything she's gone through, I'll feel like a traitor."

"Just remember," said Ethan, "we're going there to try to *help* Dottie." But he had to admit that going to the ice cream shop would feel pretty weird. *Like walking into enemy territory*, he thought as he watched Brayden disappear into his garage on that bright-red bike.

"You two slide in next to your mother," said Dad, standing beside the church pew. "I'll take the aisle seat."

Devin ducked in first, and Ethan sat between her and Dad. The church seemed especially hot today. *Are those fans working?* Ethan wondered, staring up at the ceiling.

Dad seemed extra fidgety, too. He kept twisting in his seat.

"Are you okay?" Ethan finally whispered, right in the middle of Pastor Jordan's sermon.

"Yeah, I'm fine," said Dad. "Just stretching my back."

But when Ethan leaned forward to stretch his own back, he spotted something: Dad's phone in his hand. And even from a seat away, Ethan could see the purple swirl of incense surrounding Dad's Trainer avatar.

Dad was playing Pokémon GO in church! And he was actually using incense, which meant that for the next half hour, Pokémon would visit him right here in the church pews.

Ethan laughed out loud, which he covered up with a cough. *Wow, Dad's really hooked,* he thought, shaking his head. *No wonder he wanted the aisle seat!*

He kept an eye on Dad's screen, which was a lot more interesting than Pastor Jordan's sermon. When a Pokémon popped up, he wanted to shout, "There's a Pidgey in the pew!"

But he didn't want to bust Dad.

As it turned out, he didn't have to. The sudden vibration of Dad's phone against the wooden pew made a bunch of heads turn, including Mom's.

She shot him a withering look and pointed at the phone, which he immediately turned off and slid into his pocket.

So much for that, thought Ethan.

When church finally let out, Dad was the first one out of the pew. And when Ethan asked his mom if he and Devin could walk to the ice cream shop, Dad said, "Sounds like fun! I'll go, too."

He obviously didn't want to be alone with Mom, who was still fuming. But having Dad at Ivan's Ice Cream would make it really hard to spy on Bella. So Ethan thought fast.

"We're walking there, Dad—under the hot sun. And you don't have sunscreen on. You know how fast you'll burn your head on a day like this."

It wasn't a great line, but it was the best Ethan could come up with on short notice. And Mom picked it up and ran with it.

"Yes, dear. I *really* think you should stay out of the heat and come home with me."

Dad looked like a little kid who was being tugged to the principal's office by the ear. But he waved good-bye to Ethan and Devin in the parking lot and climbed into the car with Mom.

"What was that all about?" asked Devin.

"I think Dad's going to get grounded," said

Ethan, laughing. "But don't worry about that right now. We have a mystery to solve."

As soon as Ethan and Devin got close to the ice cream shop, they spotted Bella's red bike in the bike rack. "I knew it!" he said. "She's here."

Then he pulled out his phone and tapped on the red gym to check out the competition. "Ivan's Ice Cream Shop: Gym level 3," the bar along the top read.

He scrolled through a couple of Trainers and their Pokémon. And there was Bella's blonde Trainer avatar, Bellasaur16, standing beside a nasty-looking Venusaur.

"Her Venusaur has a CP of 814!" Ethan said, tapping the screen. "And Ivan's Ice Cream is already a Level-Three gym. Dottie's is only at Level Two."

As they walked through the front door, things seemed even bleaker. The shop was packed full of kids, which the doughnut shop *never* was—except for the day they had set the lure.

The bell to the ice cream shop jingled overhead as if to announce, "Enemy alert! Team Mystic approaching!"

About seven boys' and girls' heads popped up from a booth in the corner. None of them were eating ice cream—they were all bowed over their phones. And one of them was Bella.

"Act cool," Ethan whispered to the girls as he approached the counter.

"Can we get ice cream?" asked Devin hopefully.

"Of course," said Ethan loudly. "That's why we're here, isn't it?" He hoped Devin and Gianna would both play along and not blow their cover. He also hoped he had enough money in his pocket to buy ice cream for everybody. "Do you two have any cash?" he whispered.

Devin pulled her pockets inside out, revealing absolutely nothing.

Gianna's pocket held a butterfly pupa that looked like it was about to dissolve into dust. "Oh, I wondered where that went!" she said happily. "I collect them."

Ethan sighed as he reached into his own pocket and dug out a crumpled five-dollar bill. After Devin and Gianna placed their orders, there wasn't enough left for another cone.

"Just water for me," he told the cashier, who had caterpillar-like eyebrows and a thick accent. When Ethan heard someone calling the man "Ivan," he took a step back from the counter. So this was the man who was making Dottie's life miserable! But he seemed nice enough. He winked at Ethan and handed him a chocolate chip cookie—for free.

They took seats in the bright-red booth right next to Bella and her gang.

Devin practically inhaled her peanut-butter-chocolate ice cream cone. Gianna was pretty deep into her bowl of cookie-dough ice cream, too. But Ethan suddenly had no appetite. He wrapped his cookie in a napkin for later, and kept his ears trained on the booth next to theirs.

"You should have been here," said one guy. "It was an epic battle. Five Trainers took down the gym. Team Instinct didn't stand a chance!"

"I know, I heard," said a girl. "I wanted to be there, but I didn't get back from volleyball camp till this morning."

"You missed out," said the guy. "That's all I'm saying."

"Well, I kind of wish you'd stop saying it, already," said the girl. "Shouldn't we order something?" She slid out of the booth and headed toward the counter.

When Ethan saw that it was Bella, his hopes sank. "Let's go," he said to the girls. "You can eat while we walk."

"Why?" whispered Devin. "I thought we were

spying on you know who!"

"We don't need to anymore," said Ethan with a sigh. "She's not our crook."

He was fresh out of leads and didn't know where to go next. He just knew that he wanted *out* of Ivan's Ice Cream shop.

CHAPTER 7

As Ethan walked out of the ice cream shop, he nearly ran head-on into Brayden.

"Whoa . . ." Brayden said slowly, "what are you guys doing here?" He narrowed his eyes and looked past Ethan toward the booth full of Team Valor players. "Did you come here to point the finger at my sister for that doughnut thing?"

"Don't worry about it," said Ethan, stepping around him. "We know your sister didn't do it."

"How exactly do we know that?" asked Gianna as she dumped her plastic spoon and bowl into the trash can on the sidewalk out front.

"Because she was at volleyball camp last night."

"Huh," said Devin, licking ice cream off her fingers. "We kind of told you so, didn't we? But at least the ice cream was good!"

"I wouldn't know," grumbled Ethan.

Gianna fell into step beside him. "I get why Dottie is so worried about her business," she said. "Ivan's Ice Cream was a lot busier than the doughnut shop usually is. I wish we could figure out a way to help her get more customers!"

Devin nodded—and then suddenly grabbed her vibrating phone from her pocket. "It's Pidgey!" she said. "On the fire hydrant!"

She captured the Pokémon in no time. Even Ethan was impressed by her super-straight shot. But he was surprised when the Pidgey popped back out.

"How rude!" said Devin, trying again. She recaptured the Pidgey, but as stars floated up from the Poké Ball, she scrunched up her nose. Maybe Pidgey wouldn't be one of her favorite Pokémon for much longer.

"I guess this just isn't our day," said Ethan. "We trailed another potential suspect, but still didn't catch the thief. We discovered that Ivan's Ice Cream is *way* more popular than Dottie's Doughnuts. And now, even Pidgey is giving us the slip."

As they walked toward home, he sank into a gloomy silence. Dottie's Doughnuts was up ahead, but he didn't feel like stopping in. How could they face Dottie when they had no leads on the stolen doughnuts—and when Devin was wearing a chocolate-ice-cream mustache?

Then Ethan remembered something: he might be a lousy detective, but he was also a Level-Five Trainer. And he had Pokémon to train.

The idea of fighting a gym battle at Dottie's perked him right up. He could take out all his frustrations in the gym! "Can we stop?" he asked the girls, gesturing toward the shop.

Devin shrugged.

"Sure," said Gianna, hurrying ahead.

Dottie seemed surprised to see them so early in the day. "I don't have any day-old doughnuts yet," she said. "I'm still hoping for more customers, but . . . maybe that's just wishful thinking."

"That's okay," said Devin, wiping her face clean. "We're not really hungry. We just came to see you!"

"Well, how nice," said Dottie. "Maybe you can lend me some of your expert doughnut-decorating skills."

While Devin and Gianna disappeared into the kitchen with Dottie, Ethan slid into his favorite booth. He chose Raticate to battle with this time. The ratlike Pokémon looked tough—way tougher than Zubat.

As the battle began, Ethan dodged and attacked as if his life depended on it. He imagined Brayden's face on that squealing Zubat, and pretended Zubat was wearing his stolen baseball cap. And he took Zubat down as quickly as Devin had captured Pidgey that afternoon.

But Raticate was still no match for Carlo's Sparky. That Jolteon lit up Raticate like the Fourth of July. At least Ethan got off a couple of attacks this time before losing.

That hopeless feeling settled back into the pit of his stomach—until he looked a little harder at the "You lose!" screen. His battle had raised the gym's prestige by three hundred points. And that was just enough to bump the gym to the next level: Level Three.

Ethan held his breath as he watched a spot open up for one of his Pokémon. He'd done it! Even though he had lost, he had strengthened the gym. And his reward? He was now an official Gym Defender!

But which Pokémon should he leave behind?

Ethan chewed on his fingernail, thinking. He wished Carlo were here to give him some advice, but the bench and sidewalk outside were empty— except for Mrs. Applegate across the street. The librarian was sweeping the sidewalk again, as if it were her very own porch.

Ethan's finger hovered over Raticate, slid to Pidgeotto, and then came back to Raticate. That Pokémon had the highest Combat Power, and Ethan secretly hoped Carlo would see it and be impressed. *Dream on,* he told himself as he selected Raticate to place in the gym.

When he looked up again, Mrs. Applegate was locking the front door of the library. *Why so early?* wondered Ethan. Then he remembered. It was Sunday, which meant short business hours.

The librarian carried something at her side. Was it a duffel bag? No, it looked more like a cat carrier. Ethan could just barely make out a little black head through the mesh of the carrier as it bobbled along toward the bike rack.

The library bike rack wasn't nearly as cool as the one in front of Dottie's. It was small and silver—just big enough for Mrs. Applegate's bike. She lowered the cat carrier into a basket at the back and then bent over to unlock her bike. Her *red* bike.

Ethan jumped up from his seat and called back to the kitchen. "Devin! Gianna! Come quick!"

Dottie ran out of the kitchen first, her eyes wide. "What? What is it?"

"Um, just a . . . Pokémon," fibbed Ethan,

gesturing toward the sidewalk out front.

Dottie breathed a sigh of relief. Then she said sternly, "Honestly, Ethan, you nearly gave me a heart attack. Sometimes I think you kids take that game a little too seriously."

As she turned to head back into the kitchen, Devin and Gianna appeared in the doorway. Ethan waved them into the front room and gestured toward the library.

"What?" asked Devin. Then she did a double take. "Oh, wow."

"She is so *not* the doughnut thief," whispered Gianna.

"I don't think so either," said Devin. "But you said we have to turn over every stone, or whatever."

"Actually, what I said was that we have to calmly analyze every situation," said Gianna.

"Right," said Ethan. "*Every* situation, even this one. Let's go interview Mrs. Applegate."

As they hurried across the street, Ethan kept his eyes trained on the bike. Even from a few feet away, he could see the word MILER clearly written along one of the bars. It was the same bike as Bella's! Except Mrs. Applegate's had a wire basket in back.

As he stepped onto the curb, he noticed her black cat watching him suspiciously from the carrier in that basket. Suddenly, a wave of nervousness threatened to wash Ethan away. Mrs. Applegate was so strict. What in the world were they even going to say to her?

Before he could think of something, Devin started talking. "That's a very nice bike, Mrs. Applegate!" she said. "Did you park that across the street at Dottie's a couple of days ago? I think I saw it there."

Mrs. Applegate nodded. "Yes, indeed. My bike rack gets way too full, especially on weekends. I've been after the city for a new one, but . . . well, these things take time, don't they?"

Devin nodded enthusiastically. "They do. Yep, they do." Then she seemed to lose her nerve, too. She looked to Gianna for help.

"So, Mrs. Applegate," said Gianna carefully, "do you like doughnuts? Because it must be nice having a doughnut shop right across the street!"

The librarian shook her head. "Goodness, no," she said. "With my diabetes, just *looking* at a doughnut spells trouble!"

"Oh, right," said Gianna, nodding. "Yes, I guess it would."

Well, that solves that, thought Ethan. *We found the owner of the mysterious red bike. But she's not our thief, either. We're right back to square one.*

Ethan suddenly felt tired—very, very tired. Devin and Gianna were dragging, too, as they turned to cross the street.

Maybe we should just walk away from the case, Ethan thought. *It's no big deal. It's just a tray of missing doughnuts.*

But then Mrs. Applegate said something else— something that changed everything.

"Are you kids going back to Dottie's?" she called as she strapped on her helmet. "Please tell her that I'm so sorry to hear that she's closing her shop. I don't eat the doughnuts, but I've sure enjoyed smelling them all these years. I'm going to miss her when she goes."

Closing her shop?

Ethan felt like a Pokémon who'd just been struck by Thunder Shock. Devin was saying something to him. He saw her mouth moving. But he couldn't hear a thing.

CHAPTER 8

"Why didn't she tell us?"

This time Ethan heard Devin's words. And he could see the tears welling up in her eyes.

"I don't know," he said sadly. "Should we ask her?"

But neither one of them moved.

"We should at least get out of the street," Gianna suggested as a car slowed to a crawl to go around them.

But as they filed back into the doughnut shop, Ethan couldn't bring himself to look at Dottie. It hurt too much.

"My, my," she said, wiping her hands on her apron. "Why the long faces?"

That did it. Devin burst into tears. "We h-heard!" she sobbed. "You're closing d-down!"

Dottie's face fell. She held out her arms and wrapped Devin up in them.

"Oh, sweetie," she said, smoothing back Devin's hair. "It's just time. I've had a good run, but business is too slow. I can't afford to stay open anymore, not with tough competition like Ivan's Ice Cream in town. Plus, after the break-in the other night, I just . . . I think it's time."

Ethan was about to protest. But when he saw Devin wiping her runny nose on her sleeve, he reached into his pocket—he remembered he had a napkin in there somewhere.

As he yanked it out of his pocket, a chocolate chip cookie fell to the floor. The cookie from the ice cream shop. He'd forgotten all about it!

The cookie broke into pieces, and everyone turned to stare at the napkin in Ethan's hand. The napkin that read Ivan's Ice Cream in bold, red letters.

He crumpled it up quickly, hoping Dottie hadn't seen. But it was too late.

"It's okay, Ethan," she said quietly. "I hear the ice cream at Ivan's is pretty good, actually."

Devin shook her head. "It's not!" she said. "It's terrible! I mean, it's not as good as your doughnuts. Not even close!"

Dottie gave her a sad smile. "It's like apples and oranges, isn't it? You can't really compare them. So you kids enjoy your ice cream. I don't mind." She winked at Ethan, but he still felt terrible.

He picked up the broken cookie. Then he took a deep breath and finally asked the question that had been burning in his mind. "How much longer?" he asked.

"How much longer will I stay open?" she asked. "Well, my lease is up in a month. The end of August."

One month, thought Ethan. *So we have one month to change Dottie's mind.*

"How can she just close down?" asked Devin. It was Monday morning, and she was pushing her breakfast around on her plate.

"It's grown-up stuff, honey," said Mom, ruffling her hair. "Sometimes adults have to make hard decisions. And as hard as this is for you, it's even harder for Dottie. Try to be kind to her right now, okay? Bring her a smile when you see her."

But as soon as Mom's back was turned, Devin made a face. She hid her eggs under a napkin and pushed away from the table.

Ethan couldn't blame her. His toast was sticking in his throat, and no amount of orange juice would wash it down.

Dad had already left for work, and Devin seemed determined to lock herself in her bedroom. So Ethan stepped outside and sat on the porch, scanning his Pokémon GO map for anything new.

He saw the pink petals instantly. Someone had set a lure, but where? He slid his map around so that he was facing the falling petals. Then he looked up. He could see the water tower in the distance, the word NEWVILLE painted across it, larger than life.

He'd been to that PokéStop only once. There wasn't much out there in the way of Pokémon. But with a lure, things would be different. Pokémon would be popping up every few minutes. Maybe *this* was just the thing to cheer Devin up!

He raced inside and knocked on his sister's door. He didn't know when the lure had been set. They might not have much time.

As soon as Devin saw the pink petals, her face lit up. "Let's go," she said, sliding her sandals on.

Mom agreed that they could ride their bikes to the water tower—as long as they stayed together. "And no phones out while you ride," she reminded them. "Be safe!"

Ethan tucked his phone in his pocket and strapped on his bike helmet. Then he took off down the street, with Devin matching his speed. The breeze on his face felt good, and he found himself smiling as he rode, in spite of everything that had happened over the last few days.

The water tower rose up in front of them, and Ethan could see that there were already a few kids gathered around it. One of them seemed taller than the rest—and a whole lot more bald.

"Dad?"

Ethan dropped his bike and hurried over to his father. "Aren't you supposed to be at work at the bank?"

Dad's cheeks turned a little pink when he said, "Yes, well, I'm taking a lunch break."

"At 8:30 in the morning?" asked Ethan, grinning.

Dad just shrugged. He'd been busted—again.

"Wow, there's a wild Butterfree!" said Devin, hurrying toward the bushes. Dad nearly ran out of his shoes to get to it, too.

None of them could catch the fluttering Butterfree. "Where's Gia when you need her?" said Devin with an exasperated sigh.

But the lure attracted all sorts of other Pokémon, too, from a snakelike Ekans to a poisonous Nidoran, and a cute, foxlike Vulpix. Ethan collected so many new Pokémon, he got bumped up to Level Six!

By the time the pink petals disappeared, even Devin was grinning from ear to ear. "That was *so* fun!" she said, climbing back onto her bike.

Dad straightened out his tie and walked to his car. Before he got in, he cleared his throat and said to Ethan, "About this morning . . ."

Ethan pretended to zip his lips shut. "Mum's the word, Dad," he said. "I mean, I won't tell Mum—er, Mom."

Dad smiled wide and nodded. "Good boy," he said, ducking into the car. He rolled his window down, and Ethan could hear him humming as he started to drive away.

Riding back home, Ethan rode much more slowly. Devin did, too, stopping now and then to explore fields for Pokémon.

As they passed the nature preserve, Ethan almost asked Devin if she wanted to walk the trail. It was a good day for it—not too hot, and not much else to do. But someone shouted to them from across the street.

"Hey, Team Mystic!" called Brayden from his scooter. "Defend your gym much?"

He grinned at them, but something about that smile sent a cold chill down Ethan's spine. As Brayden disappeared into his garage, Ethan wondered, *What did he mean by that?*

"Devin," he said. "We'd better get to Dottie's. And fast."

They biked full speed ahead—past the softball fields and the Laundromat. Devin fell behind, but Ethan couldn't slow down. As soon as he reached the library, he whipped out his phone.

When he looked at the screen, his heart sank to the pit of his stomach.

Dottie's Doughnuts gym, which had been Team Mystic's blue all summer, was no longer blue.

It was blood red.

Team *Valor* red.

CHAPTER 9

Ethan spotted Carlo sitting on the bench by Dottie's front door. For once, he wasn't staring at his phone.

When they locked eyes, Carlo said, "Hey, Ethan."

Wow, he actually knows my name, thought Ethan. When he got closer, he said, "I can't believe Team Valor stole the gym. What are you going to do now?"

Carlo ran his hand over his dark hair. "There's not much I can do," he said with a sigh. "There are four Team Valor Defenders here, all with strong Pokémon. Bella's Aerodactyl has a Combat Power of 1216! I don't think I can beat them all. There's too many of them."

Ethan had never heard Carlo sound so gloomy. Where was the bold, cocky Carlo who walked around like he owned the place? *Come on,* Ethan wanted to say. *Let's fight! Let's get the gym back!*

Carlo took a deep breath and blew it back out. "It's funny," he said, almost to himself. "Bella and her team didn't care about this gym at all for weeks. Then all of a sudden, they ganged up and attacked. What's up with that?"

Ethan felt a niggle of guilt. He knew at least one reason why Team Valor might have come after the gym; it had something to do with a red bike and a few accusations.

Brayden probably told Bella we were spying on her at the ice cream shop—in front of a whole group of Team Valor kids! he realized. But he couldn't tell Carlo that.

As Carlo pushed up from the bench and waved good-bye, Ethan tried to swallow the Poké Ball-sized lump in his throat.

"Is he going to get Dottie's gym back?" asked Devin as she finished locking her bike to the rack outside Dottie's Doughnuts. Her cheeks were flushed red.

"I don't think so," Ethan said sadly.

"What? He has to!" exclaimed Devin. "For Dottie! Maybe if you help him win back the gym, Dottie will know how much we care about her shop, and she'll keep it open."

Ethan thought that was a pretty big *maybe*. But her words stirred the fire in his chest.

"Carlo says he can't do it alone," he said, thinking out loud. "But maybe if we help him—if we *all* help him . . ."

An hour later, they were sitting on Gianna's porch. Ethan was surprised to see that Gianna had convinced Carlo to join them.

"You don't have to do it alone, Carlo," she said again. "There were three Team Mystic Trainers defending the gym. You don't have to fight for it all by yourself. Do it as a team!"

Carlo shook his head. "You don't understand. I don't even know who BatGirl is, and Ethan, well . . ."

He didn't finish his sentence, so Ethan finished it for him. "I'm just a beginner," he said. "I know. Me and my Raticate aren't much help." Then that fire flared up again in his chest, and he added, "But you could teach me. If we work together, we can do this. I know we can!"

Carlo didn't look so sure.

Then Gianna stood up and took a deep breath. "I have a confession to make," she said. "I know who BatGirl is."

Ethan whirled around. "Really?" he said. "You know who was defending Dottie's gym with that fierce Zubat?"

Gianna nodded. She stared at the tips of her shoes when she said, "It's me."

Carlo scoffed. "You don't even have a phone!"

"And your Trainer name isn't BatGirl. It's Giadude!" said Devin.

Gianna shrugged. "Dottie lent me her phone sometimes when I stopped by to visit. And I have two accounts and Trainer names because . . . I kind of didn't want Carlo to know I was training at his gym." She turned toward her brother and said, "I thought you wouldn't want me around. I mean, you usually don't."

"Why not?" asked Carlo, raising his hands at his sides. "You're good!"

"Yeah, you are," said Ethan. "I should know—I battled you twice."

Carlo grinned at Gianna. "Maybe you take after me, little sis."

She punched him in the shoulder. "No thanks

to you," she said. "You never taught me anything. You wouldn't help me at all!"

Carlo's face fell. "You're right," he said. "I didn't." He stared off into the distance for a moment and then said, "That's going to have to change if we're going to win the gym back."

"So you'll try?" asked Gianna, jumping up.

He nodded. "But we're going to need lots of Trainers and powerful Pokémon. And pretty much the only place we can train is at the library—that's the closest Team Mystic gym now."

Ethan groaned. "Mrs. Applegate will chase us right out of there!"

Carlo smiled. "I might know a couple of secret spots where we can hide out," he said thoughtfully.

"Can I help, too?" asked Devin. "I mean, I know I've never battled before, but I could learn."

"Hey, you could evolve some of your Pidgey!" exclaimed Ethan. "You could end up with a Pidgeot with pretty high Combat Power that way. I mean, only if you want to, though." He remembered her words: *You play your way, I'll play mine.*

Devin took a deep breath. "I do love my Pidgey," she said. "But I love Dottie's Doughnuts even more."

"Good," said Ethan. "So, are we really doing

this?" He gazed at his circle of friends and then held out his hand, palm down.

Devin put hers on top of his right away. Gianna added her own hand, and then looked at Carlo. He hesitated for just a moment before adding his hand to the pile.

"Team Mystic?" asked Ethan.

"Team Mystic!"

CHAPTER 10

"The first thing we have to do is get you to Level Five," Ethan announced to Devin when they got back home. "You need experience points—and lots of them."

He set to work helping her evolve her Pidgey into Pidgeotto, and then into one really strong Pidgeot. "He's actually pretty cute," said Devin, staring at the Pokémon who burst out of the evolution ball.

"No he's not!" said Ethan. "Take that back. He's fierce. He's powerful. He's going to win back Dottie's gym. Right?"

Devin laughed. "Right."

While they were at it, Ethan healed his Raticate, which was pretty beaten down from its battle with Team Valor at Dottie's Doughnuts.

Next, Ethan evolved one of his Weedle into a Kakuna, and then into a Beedrill. It wasn't as satisfying as *catching* a Beedrill would be, but it was still pretty exciting to see the Beedrill in his inventory. "It sure takes an awful lot of Larrys to make a Beedrill," he said to himself, chuckling.

"Huh?" asked Devin.

"Never mind. Let's stay focused."

They still had a long way to go to get Devin to Level Five, so Ethan racked his brain to remember all the ways to earn experience points. "You should try hatching a few eggs," he said. "If you hatch a new kind of Pokémon, you'll get, like, a thousand points."

Devin put a couple of eggs in her incubators, and as soon as Dad got home from work, Ethan met him in the hallway. "Time for our family walk," Ethan said. "And you'd better wear comfy shoes tonight!"

He and Devin led the walk around the block, through the nature preserve, and then around the block *again*. "What's gotten into you two?" asked Mom. "I love this energy!"

Ethan just shrugged. He could tell Mom that

they were doing this for Dottie, but she'd probably say something like, "That's grown-up stuff, honey. You shouldn't get your hopes up."

So instead, he told her that he and Devin were going for their silver Jogger medals, too. They'd probably get them pretty soon, at this rate!

But on Tuesday morning, on the way back from the grocery store, Mom caught Devin shaking her phone in the back seat. "What are you doing?" she asked.

"Logging steps," Devin admitted. "Maybe if I shake my phone like this, the app will *think* I'm walking!"

Ethan tried to get her to stop talking. He put his hands up in a T shape, like a time-out signal, but she kept on yammering away about the cool new trick she'd discovered. And just as Ethan predicted, Mom got mad.

"Devin, that's cheating!" she scolded, bringing the car to a screeching halt. "Now you can either hand over your phone, young lady, or you and Ethan can hop out of the car and walk home. Get those steps in honestly. Which will it be?"

Devin shrugged and hopped out, which Ethan thought was kind of unfair. Why did he have to walk, too?

Then he thought about Dottie's Doughnut

shop and remembered they were all in this together. *Team Mystic,* he told himself. So he followed his sister out of the car and started walking.

"Where did Carlo say we should meet?" whispered Devin.

"Back here somewhere," said Ethan, stepping over a pothole. They were in the alleyway behind the library, which was dark and littered with trash.

"Do you think rats live in this alley?" asked Devin, giving the dumpster a wide berth.

Ethan shrugged. "Hopefully there's a Rattata or two," he joked.

"Hey, guys!" Gianna's voice echoed throughout the tunnellike alley. It was followed by a loud hushing noise, which meant Carlo was with her.

He waved Ethan and Devin toward the crumbling staircase that led to the back door of the library. "Let's sit here," he said. "We're close enough to the gym to train, but Mrs. Applegate never uses this door."

Ethan glanced up at the cobweb-filled window next to the door. He hoped Carlo was right about Mrs. Applegate. She wasn't big on kids playing

Pokémon GO anywhere near the library, and right now, they were about as near to the library as they could be without actually being *in* it.

"Are you all ready to train?" asked Carlo, rubbing his hands together. "Because I've got every tip and trick you need."

Ethan was glad to see that brave, confident Carlo was back. With him as their leader, they couldn't lose!

Carlo handed Gianna his phone, and they all tapped on the blue gym tower on their screens. The library was a Level-One Team Mystic gym, led by none other than Carlo.

I guess he's the only kid brave enough to play here at the library, thought Ethan.

But soon, the three of them were taking turns engaging in friendly battles with Carlo's Fearow. He showed Devin the basics, like swiping left or right to dodge an attack. But he gave Ethan and Gianna some insider tricks.

"Fearow is a Flying-type Pokémon," he reminded them. "So fight it with a Pokémon that has high Combat Power, but is also strong against Flying-types—like Grass, Fighting, or Bug."

"Like Beedrill?" asked Gianna, scrolling through her Pokémon.

"Exactly."

Then he showed Ethan how to perform one

of Raticate's Special Attacks. "Wait till your blue attack bar starts getting full," he said, pointing to the blue bar in the upper left of the screen. "Then press down on my Fearow with your finger. Now! There, see? You did it!"

"Raticate did Hyper Beam!" shouted Ethan, pumping his fist as Fearow disappeared in a feathery *poof*.

When he realized his battle had bumped the library up to a Level-Two gym, he was even more excited. "Can I leave my Raticate here?" he asked Carlo.

"No!" said Carlo right away. "You need to keep him for our *real* battle, against Team Valor. You need six strong Pokémon to fight a rival gym. So leave one of your less powerful Pokémon here."

Ethan chose a Spearow, which Devin happily fought in her next battle. When she *beat* the Spearow with her Pidgeot, even Ethan was happy for her.

While Gianna was training her Beedrill, he leaned back against the brick wall, healing his tired Pokémon with Potion. That's when he heard a strange mewing sound. "Are you battling with Meowth?" he asked Gianna.

"Shh! I'm trying to concentrate!" she said, keeping her eyes glued to her phone.

"That's not coming from the game," said Carlo, standing up. He stepped carefully around the dumpster, searching the shadows.

Then Ethan heard the sound again, coming from *above* them. He glanced up at the cobweb-covered window and saw a black cat pressed against the screen. Mrs. Applegate's cat!

"Shh, Max, be quiet," Carlo called up to it, as if he and the cat were old friends.

But Max wasn't quiet. His meowing grew louder and more agitated. He pawed at the window. And then suddenly he was whisked away, and another face appeared.

Mrs. Applegate.

CHAPTER 11

Ethan fought the urge to run. It would be pointless now. Mrs. Applegate had already seen them!

"Carlo, what did I tell you about playing that game out here?" she said, shaking a finger at him through the window. She disappeared for a moment, and Ethan heard the *click* of the back door unlocking.

When Mrs. Applegate stepped outside, she didn't look happy—not one bit. "The library is for reading, not video games. Now, if you kids want to come in here and check out a book, I'm happy to help you. Otherwise, I suggest you move along."

"Yes, Mrs. Applegate," said Carlo, bowing his head. He took his phone from Gianna and led everyone down the littered alley and out into the sunshine.

"Well, so much for that," said Ethan, sitting on the curb across from Dottie's Doughnuts. "But we learned a lot! Do you think we're ready?"

Carlo sighed. "I don't know. But we might have to be. I don't know where else we can train."

Ethan took one more look at his Pokémon. Raticate was now fully healed. "I feel ready," he said, standing up.

"Me, too," said Devin, even though she looked pretty nervous.

"I'm ready," said Gianna. "I just need a phone. . . . Do you think Dottie would lend me hers for the battle?"

"If she knew you were trying to save the doughnut shop, she would!" said Devin. "You should ask her."

Gianna nodded. "I will."

"So, when are we doing this?" asked Ethan.

Everyone turned to Carlo, who ran his hand over his hair. "Tomorrow," he said firmly. "Wednesday afternoons are dead at the doughnut shop. That's when Ivan debuts his new ice cream flavors with free samples. Between two and two-thirty, Team Valor will flock there like a bunch of Pidgeys."

Ethan chewed on a fingernail. Just the thought of doing battle with Team Valor tomorrow made his stomach flip-flop. But there was no use putting it off. Every day they waited, Dottie got closer to hanging a CLOSED sign in her shop window.

"Two o'clock tomorrow," he echoed. *We're doing this. And we're going to win—we* have *to win.*

"Something's wrong with Mom," Devin whispered, poking her ginger-red head through Ethan's doorway.

"What do you mean?"

"I don't know. She's acting weird. Are we in trouble for doing something that I forgot about?"

Ethan laughed. "No, she's probably just stressed about work or something."

But at dinner that night, Ethan realized how wrong he was.

The first thing Mom said was, "How was the library today?"

Uh-oh. Ethan shot Devin a look, but she was playing with her peas.

"Um, fine," he said, answering for them both.

"How many books did you check out?" asked Mom.

Ethan shrugged. Was that a trick question?

Then Mom launched into her speech. She really let them have it. "I ran into Mrs. Applegate on the sidewalk, and she informed me that you did *not* check out any books. You were battling Pokémon, which she strictly forbids at the library—which you're very well aware of. So I think it's time to set some restrictions on when and where you play the game."

No! Ethan looked to Dad for help, but Dad was shoveling potatoes into his mouth so fast, he looked like he was going to hurt himself.

Devin was no help either. She kept sinking lower and lower in her chair, until just her eyes peered over her plate.

"From now on," said Mom, "you may play for one hour in the morning. You will explore the neighborhood on *foot,* not on your bikes or in the backseat of my car. And not at church." She gave Dad a withering look. "You will pass the Little Library, where you'll each take one book to read. And then you'll return home, and I'll collect your phones for the rest of the day—until our evening walk."

"What? Mom, no!" said Ethan, dropping his fork. "You can't do that!"

Mom silenced him with her eyes. "I *can* do that, and I will. And if you take that tone with me again, you won't be allowed to have your phone at all. Understand?"

Ethan couldn't look at her. He felt like his chest was going to explode at any second. Getting his phone taken away was one thing. But Mom's timing stunk. *We need our phones tomorrow at two o'clock. Or Carlo and Gianna will battle Team Valor alone. And they'll lose. And it'll be our fault!*

When he felt hot tears filling his eyes, he couldn't take it anymore. He pushed away from the table and ran to his room.

Ethan woke to a grumbling stomach. He'd pretty much missed dinner, and then slept through breakfast, too. He wasn't going to give Mom the satisfaction of eating the blueberry pancakes he could smell through the crack in his bedroom door. Hopefully, the special breakfast meant she felt guilty about the blow-up last night. *Hopefully* it meant she would change her mind.

But no such luck. By mid-morning, Ethan still hadn't left his room. And Mom hadn't come to talk to him like he thought she would.

Devin did, though. "What are we going to do?" she whispered as she sat on the edge of his bed.

Ethan shrugged. "What *can* we do?"

His sister listed the possibilities, counting them off on her fingers. "Um, run away and never come back. Or rebel and try to take over the house. Or find Mom's hiding place for our phones, and sneak out at two o'clock."

"Devin!" Ethan looked at her with new eyes. "You wouldn't do something like that."

She sighed. "Well, I don't *want* to get in trouble. But this is important! Carlo and Gianna need us. Dottie needs us, too."

They locked eyes, and that's when Ethan knew. They were actually doing this.

He only hoped they could find their phones in time.

CHAPTER 12

Mom left for her job at the real estate office at one o'clock.

Ethan expected her to come into his room to say good-bye, or to say she was sorry, or at least to offer him some lunch, but she didn't. When he heard the garage door open and close, his empty stomach sank with it.

She's not going to back down this time, he realized.

The first thing he did was run to the fridge and scarf down some ice-cold blueberry pancakes. Then he heard Devin in the hall.

"Where do you think Mom hid our phones?" she asked. "In the Christmas closet?"

Mom had a not-so-secret hiding place for Christmas gifts. A few years ago—when he was way younger—Ethan had actually snuck into the closet and opened a gift early.

"Yeah, that closet is a good guess," he said. "Let's go look."

The closet was beneath the basement stairs. The door was hard to open—it kind of scraped against the carpet. And when Ethan did finally get it open, he could barely see past the paper bags of clothing piled inside.

"Jeepers, looks like a thrift store in here," he said. "Are these clothes we've outgrown or something?"

He pulled the bags out of the closet and lined them up against the wall. Then he and Devin searched the closet from top to bottom. They found a broken vacuum cleaner, some sports trophies, and three boxes of Dad's old vinyl records, but no phones.

"Bummer," said Devin, pulling a cobweb out of her hair. "So where do we look next? In Mom's bedroom?"

Ethan's stomach twisted. His parents' bedroom was strictly off-limits, which made it a scary place to be. But it was also the perfect place for Mom to hide something.

"It might be there," he admitted. "But she'd

kill us if we dug through her stuff, and we're going to be in enough trouble already. Let's check the kitchen and office first."

As Devin took off up the stairs, he piled the paper bags back into the closet. The last thing they needed was Mom finding out they'd been digging in the Christmas closet, even if it was only July.

As he stuffed the last bag inside, something caught his eye. A Poké Ball! Was it a T-shirt? A gift for him?

He reached into the bag—and pulled out a Poké Ball cap. *His* Poké Ball cap. The one he had accused Brayden of stealing.

Whoa.

Ethan squatted down. He suddenly felt sick to his stomach.

"Are you coming or what?" Devin called from upstairs.

He swallowed hard and set the cap back in the bag. What else could he do with it right now? There was no time to think—they had to find their phones. He shut the closet door tightly and hurried up the stairs.

Mom's office was littered with real estate postings and file folders. He opened her desk drawers and looked underneath the piles of papers, all the while trying not to think about that cap.

He heard Devin banging around in the kitchen, too. But after forty-five minutes of searching the kitchen, the office, the basement, and even the garage, they'd found nothing!

Devin asked again, "Should we check the bedroom? Mom knows it's the last place we'd look."

Ethan glanced at the clock on the wall. They had only fifteen minutes now to find the phones and get to the doughnut shop. They couldn't be late—not today. But searching through Mom and Dad's bedroom felt just as weird and wrong as walking into Ivan's Ice Cream shop had a few days ago.

He chewed his fingernail and stared at the bookcase in the hall. "Actually, Mom probably thinks the last place we'd look is on a bookshelf," he said with a grin. "She thinks we're not reading enough this summer, remember?"

He stood on tiptoe and slid his hand along the top of the bookshelf.

No one was as shocked as Ethan when his fingers tripped over something hard and flat. He slid it forward until it teetered on the edge of the shelf. "My phone!"

Devin jumped up and down. "Is mine up there, too?"

Sure enough, it was. Ethan slid it off, handed it

to her, and then checked the time on his phone. It read 1:49. "We gotta go," he said. "Now!"

He ran toward the front door and slid into his sneakers. But when he put his hand on the doorknob, he was surprised to feel it turn in his hand.

Did Mom come back? he thought with horror. He held the knob firmly for a moment, as if he could keep her outside—out of the way of his and Devin's plan.

But as the knob started to slip in his sweaty hand, he felt his hopes for a Team Mystic victory slip away, too.

CHAPTER 13

As the door swung open, Ethan braced himself. But it wasn't Mom standing on the front steps. It was *Dad*, who jumped back in surprise and nearly stumbled down them.

"Ethan!" he said, grabbing the stair rail. "Why were you blocking the door?"

"Because . . ." Ethan confessed, "I thought you were Mom."

That's when he decided to tell Dad everything—about Team Valor taking over the doughnut shop gym, and Dottie deciding to close the store, and Carlo and Gianna meeting there *right now* to try to save it. Devin chimed in to help him tell the story.

It was two o'clock when Ethan and Devin finished spilling their guts to Dad in the doorway. It was ten minutes later when Dad finally agreed to let them go.

Maybe it was because Ethan brought up the water tower incident, when he'd promised to cover for Dad so Mom wouldn't know he had skipped work to hunt Pokémon. Or maybe Dad just had a soft spot for Dottie's Doughnuts.

"I'll drive you," he said, jingling his keys. "Let's go!"

Ethan held his breath all the way there. *Are we too late?* he worried and wondered.

But as Dad pulled to a stop in front of the doughnut shop, Ethan could tell from the map on his phone that the Team Valor gym was in the thick of battle. The top of the gym was *exploding* with lightning, fire, wind, and clouds.

"We have to get in there!" he hollered to Devin. "Now!"

Sure enough, Carlo and Gianna had started battling without them.

As Ethan slid into the booth, Gianna didn't look up—she couldn't take her eyes away from her screen. "We thought you weren't coming!" she cried.

"We came!" said Ethan. "We're here." *We're probably grounded for life, but we're here.*

"We need your help," said Carlo. "Choose your top six Pokémon. Hurry!" His forehead was sweating, and he was furiously tapping his screen.

Ethan felt his own heart race as he pulled up his Pokémon. He chose his six most powerful, and then he entered the battle. His Raticate popped up, ready to face off against a Team Valor Venonat.

Ethan scanned the screen. The number three below Raticate's health meter showed that three friends were battling by his side. And across the battle arena, he could see Carlo's Sparky. He was battling *with* Sparky instead of against him this time, and that gave Ethan courage.

When the word "Go!" flashed across the screen, he dodged the bouncy, purple Venonat's first attack. Then Raticate snarled and started fighting back.

Ethan tapped the screen until the blue attack bar was almost full. Then he pressed and held his finger on Venonat to deliver Raticate's Hyper Beam, which blew Venonat to smithereens.

"Victory!" the screen said.

"Yes!" cried Ethan.

But there wasn't much time to celebrate. Team Valor's Doduo was already in place, ready for battle number two.

Ethan swiped left to dodge Doduo's attack. Then he tapped the screen over and over again. "Take that, you two-headed monster!" Finally, he pressed his finger against Doduo until Raticate delivered a perfect Dig.

Yes! Another win! Ethan could hardly believe it.

The next Team Valor Pokémon popped up for battle.

It was a Lickitung, but its nickname was "Licks." When Ethan saw the Trainer name below it, his stomach dropped.

Brayboy.

Ethan swallowed hard. He was about to battle Brayden. And all the guilt he'd felt about finding that Poké Ball cap in the closet came rushing back.

We wouldn't even be fighting Team Valor if I hadn't accused Brayden of being a thief, he thought. *It's all my fault. So I have to win this. I have to!*

As soon as the battle began, Ethan's hands started sweating like crazy. He tried to dodge Licks's attack, but his finger slipped. Raticate's own attacks were too slow. And Lickitung was too powerful.

Poof! Raticate was gone.

Ethan could barely breathe.

When his Pidgeotto popped onto the screen, he

tried to focus. *Get it together*, he told himself. *Your friends are counting on you!*

But his phone was so slippery now, he accidentally dropped it. And Licks made another quick attack.

Poof! Pidgeotto was gone.

Poof! Poof! Poof! Poof! Ethan's last four battles were a blur. One after another, his Pokémon fainted.

"You lose!" the screen screamed at him.

Ethan turned his phone upside down and slumped in his seat.

He'd never even gotten to battle Bella's Aerodactyl. He had started the fight with Team Valor, but he wasn't good enough or strong enough to finish it. Ethan wished *he* could disappear in a puff of smoke, too.

Devin gave him a sympathetic smile. She'd been done playing for a while now, but Carlo and Gianna were still fighting.

"At least we helped a little," Devin pointed out. "See?" She held up her own "You lose!" screen, which showed that the gym's prestige had gone down by a hundred points.

Ethan had a sinking suspicion that it wouldn't be enough—until Carlo jumped up with a whoop!

"We did it!" he hollered. "Grab your phones—we

need to take control of the gym and get our Pokémon in there before another team does. Hurry!"

When Ethan whipped his phone over, the gym on his map was gray—unclaimed, at least for now. He tried to think fast. Which Pokémon should he put in there?

He finally chose Raticate. *You fought a tough battle, buddy,* he thought. *It's not your fault I totally fell apart.*

Then Ethan saw something that made him smile wide. The gym on his map had turned blue again. Bright, beautiful blue.

When he tapped on it, he saw "Dottie's Doughnuts, Level Four." And as he swiped through the trainer information, he saw each of his friends and their finest Pokémon.

There was DevGirl506, with Pidgeot by her side. Giadude99 had placed her Beedrill in the gym. And there was Carlozard14 with Sparky, the crowned Gym Leader once more.

Everything's okay, thought Ethan. *I almost ruined it, but everything turned out okay.*

When he looked up from his phone, he realized that Dad and Dottie had been watching from a nearby booth.

"You did it!" said Dad.

"Go Team Mystic!" Dottie cheered.

"Whew! That was tough," said Carlo. "Remember to use Revives to heal any Pokémon that fainted. They worked hard today."

"You kids did, too," said Dottie. "I think this calls for doughnuts!"

As she headed for the kitchen, Gianna called after her. "Do you have any powdered-sugar ones?"

"Ooh, and those ones with purple sprinkles?" asked Devin.

"And those Jigglypuffs?" added Carlo. "Those are my new favorite."

Ethan couldn't think of his own favorite doughnut. He couldn't even think about the battle they'd just won.

Why? Because an idea had just flickered in his brain, like a PokéStop spinning in a circle when he'd finally stepped close enough to activate it.

Ethan was pretty sure he'd just solved the Case of the Stolen Jigglypuffs.

CHAPTER 14

"Now that we got the gym back, you'll keep the shop open, won't you Dottie?" asked Devin, taking a big bite of her purple doughnut.

"Oh, sweetie," said Dottie, putting her hand on Devin's shoulder. "You know, I love what you kids did today. But I didn't realize you were hoping . . ."

"Wait, you're still going to close?" asked Gianna, her eyes wide. "But we worked so hard!"

Dottie sighed. "Oh, dear. You fought that battle today for me?"

Gianna nodded sadly and set her powdered doughnut on her napkin.

Ethan knew just how she felt. His doughnut suddenly didn't taste so fresh.

Dottie took a deep breath. "You know, ever since the shop was broken into, I haven't felt the same way about it. It doesn't feel safe here. It doesn't feel like home anymore."

"Wait, the shop was broken into?" asked Carlo. "When?"

"You didn't know?" said Dottie, her eyes wide. "I thought you were all working together to try to solve that mystery!"

Gianna shook her head. "Not Carlo. He didn't start working with us at all until just a couple of days ago—to win back the gym."

"But what was stolen?" asked Carlo.

Ethan watched him closely as Dottie described the missing tray of Jigglypuffs. And the shock on Carlo's face told him everything he needed to know.

Carlo opened his mouth and then shut it again. He looked like he was struggling to find words.

So Ethan helped him out. "Did you take the doughnuts, Carlo?" he asked in a quiet voice.

Carlo's face collapsed. "I did! I mean, I didn't *steal* them! I came in hoping Dottie had some day-old doughnuts, and she did—that tray of Jigglypuffs. And then I accidentally knocked the tray onto the floor, so I tried to clean it up and not leave a mess.

I didn't know where Dottie was, and . . . I—I was embarrassed. I'm so sorry." He hung his head.

Devin whirled around to face Ethan. "How'd you know Carlo did it?" she asked.

Ethan shrugged. "He said Jigglypuffs were his favorite. But Dottie only made them that one time, and Carlo wasn't helping out with that sale. So when would he have tried them? Unless . . . he was the one who came back into the shop that night."

"But the door was unlocked!" said Carlo. "I thought Dottie was still here!"

Devin sighed. "That was my fault," she said. "I forgot to lock it."

Dottie's face spread into a slow smile. "It's nobody's fault," she said. "In fact, I'm suddenly feeling a whole lot better."

Carlo slumped in his seat. "But now I feel lousy," he said. "What can I do to make it right?"

Gianna's head popped up. "I have an idea. You're a Level-Twelve Trainer, right, Carlo?"

"Actually, Level Thirteen," he mumbled.

"So you get lure modules as rewards some-times, right?"

He nodded.

"You should set lures for Dottie! It would help her business. That's how you can make up for the Jigglypuffs!"

Carlo looked to Dottie, who shrugged. "It definitely helps business," she said with a smile.

"Okay!" said Carlo. "I can do that. When?"

"Saturday," said Dottie. "Let's try it again on Saturday. And I'll make an extra tray of Jigglypuffs, just for you." She winked.

"Are you going to tell Mom?" asked Devin as Dad drove them home.

He glanced at her in the rearview mirror. "What do you think?"

Her shoulders sagged. "I think you probably will."

"But you'll stick up for us, right, Dad?" asked Ethan. "I mean, you know *why* we disobeyed her rules."

Dad nodded. "I do. But rules are still rules."

Ethan thought that was a pretty crummy thing to say for a guy who had been playing Pokémon GO in church. But he kept his mouth shut. He really needed Dad on his side right now.

All through dinner, Ethan kept waiting for Dad to tell Mom what they'd done. He knew Devin was waiting for it, too—he could tell by the way she was making little mountains out of her mashed potatoes instead of eating them.

But Dad waited right up till the moment when Mom pulled on her sneakers for the family walk. She reached for the phones in her "secret" hiding place—the top of the bookshelf—and came up empty.

As soon as Mom's eyebrows scrunched together, Ethan darted behind Dad for protection.

"Now, honey," said Dad, holding up his hand. "Why don't we talk about this while we walk."

So Dad talked all the way past the park, all the way to the Little Library. While he rambled on, Ethan made a big show about taking a book out of the Little Library. But Mom didn't even notice.

By the time they'd reached the Pheasant Ranch trailhead, Dad had run out of things to say. But he must have explained everything totally wrong, because Mom looked *furious.*

"You allowed the kids to break my rules—and you skipped out of work this afternoon—so that they could play a *game* with their friends?" she said to Dad, whose face was now beet red.

"But, Mom, it's not just a game!" said Ethan. Why couldn't she understand that?

"It *is* just a game," Mom insisted. "That's what I've been trying to teach you kids. There are more important things than . . ." When her phone suddenly buzzed, she paused to glance at it.

That's when Mom's furious face broke into a smile.

"My medal! My medal! My silver Jogger medal!" She sang it instead of saying it. Then she danced in a circle, holding up her phone to show off her award.

Ethan glanced in both directions, hoping none of his friends were around to see this! But he couldn't help smiling, too.

"So," said Devin, giving Mom a sly grin, "what were you saying about this *game*, Mom?"

Mom was trying her hardest to keep a straight face—Ethan could tell. But she just couldn't. "Oh, never mind," she said. "Let's go hatch some Pokémon. I've got a gold medal to earn!"

With that, she took off walking. Dad gave Ethan a secret thumbs-up, and then he pulled his phone out, too.

"Listen to the birds!" Mom called over her shoulder as she walked. "Do you hear them, Ethan?"

"I hear them," he said, laughing. He also heard something else: the whine of a puppy.

That meant Brayden was nearby. So Ethan took a deep breath and turned around. There was something he had to do.

Brayden was in front of his house, tossing the puppy a tiny orange ball. He seemed surprised to see Ethan coming *toward* him instead of hurrying away from him.

"Hey," said Ethan, summoning up his courage.

"What do *you* want?" Brayden wasn't going to make this easy.

"I just wanted to tell you that I found my Poké Ball cap. So, I'm really sorry that I accused you of stealing it. I shouldn't have done that. I was wrong."

It seemed to take Brayden a second to understand what Ethan was saying. Then his face spread into a smug smile.

I deserve that, thought Ethan, even though it was hard not to look away.

Now that he had said what he needed to say, it was time to tell Brayden what he *wanted* to say. "I'm sorry about Dottie's Doughnuts, too. You guys gave it a really good shot."

Brayden's face fell like a cake in the oven. "What do you . . ." he started to ask. Then he scooped up the puppy. "I've gotta go." He hurried into the house, probably in search of Bella.

Devin giggled from the sidewalk behind Ethan. "He didn't know we won the gym back!" she said. "Did you see his face?"

"I saw it," said Ethan, grinning. "I almost feel kind of bad." *Almost.*

As he started to walk back toward the trailhead

sign, Devin fell into step beside him. "So, Brayden didn't steal your cap?"

"Nah," said Ethan. "He did steal my puppy name, but that's okay—I'm over it. I'm going to think of an even better one."

"Like what?" she asked.

When Ethan heard a commotion from behind, he stopped and turned. It was Gianna, jogging down the sidewalk. And this time, Carlo was right behind her.

As Ethan watched his teammates hurrying to catch up, the name came to him—the perfect name.

"There's only one name we can give that puppy," he said slowly. "Only one name that fits."

"What is it?" said Devin, bouncing up and down on her toes. "Tell me already. I can't stand it!"

He smiled and said, "*Mystic*. When we get our puppy, Devin, we're going to name it Mystic."

Do you Love pLaying Pokémon GO?

Check out these books for fans of Pokémon GO!

Catching the
Jigglypuff Thief
ALEX POLAN

Following Meowth's
Footprints
ALEX POLAN

Coming Soon!

Chasing Butterfree
ALEX POLAN

Cracking the
Magikarp Code
ALEX POLAN

Available wherever books are sold!